ORANGUTANKA

ORANGUTANKA

A Story in Poems

Margarita Engle

illustrated by Renée Kurilla

HENRY HOLT AND COMPANY
NEW YORK

A Note About Tanka Poems

Orangutanka is written as a series of linked tanka poems known as a "string" of tanka.

Tanka is an ancient Japanese form consisting of five lines, with a traditional syllable count of 5, 7, 5, 7, 7. Modern tanka poets rarely count syllables, but do follow a basic line pattern of short, long, short, long, long. The poems in this book take the modern approach and mostly have a loose line length structure rather than adhering to strict syllable counts.

The tanka form is often used as a poetic travel diary. Unlike haiku, tanka poems can include simile, metaphor, opinions, emotions, and, occasionally, a bit of rhyme.

Tanka poems are traditionally untitled, with minimal punctuation and capitalization.

After reading *Orangutanka*, consider inviting children to create their own tanka poems about any topic at all!

cozy morning
baby orangutan cuddles
with mama
in their leafy nest
while a breeze sways green trees

sleepy mama
wants to keep resting
in the nest
but baby and big sister
peek over the edge

papa
is too massive
for treetops—
his great weight makes
low branches waltz slowly

big sister
leaps and clings, swings

on vines,

flips, dips, swoops, twirls,

and smiles upside down

heaps of sweet fruit
are piled up on a platform—
such wild excitement
as forest rangers offer
a feast for orangutans!

towering green trees
shiver, sway, rattle, and shake
when orangutans
clamber toward colorful mounds
of bananas and mangoes

touching

a ranger's hand

big sister

chooses a golden pineapple

while grandma eats orange melons

riding happily
on mama's soft, furry back
curious baby
watches the dazzling fruit feast
and discovers butterflies

in afternoon heat
sly, mischievous big sister
sneaks all the way down
from an enormous tree's height
to explore the forest floor

hip-hop somersaults and cartwheels, cha-cha-cha—

so many forms of orangudance with lively arms and legs

one eye open

alert grandma watches

sister's dance

while the rest of the family naps

dreaming orangutan dreams

rain—
the adventure
grows soggy

time for a big, floppy
green-leaf umbrella

alone
on a noisy road
surrounded
by chattering humans
sister wishes for treetops

high up
mama relaxes in her nest
resting
while baby plays
with raindrops

papa
smacks his lips
hungry
even though he is still
peacefully sleeping

only grandma

dares to climb down to the ground

and join

sister's joyful, flip-flop,

acrobatic road dance

safe in a treetop
with brave, gentle old grandma
sister has a chance
to glance down at the children
who dance like orangutans!

An Orangudance Activity

imagine

rain forest music—

insects

buzz, zoom, and hum

while green leaves swish

twigs rattle

branches drum, and thunder booms—

can YOU dance

like a happy orangutan

with energetic arms and legs?

Orangutan Facts

- Orangutans are found only in the rain forests of Borneo and Sumatra.

- Orangutans live almost entirely in the trees. In the Malay language, *orangutan* means "forest person."

- Wild adult orangutans spend most of their time alone, searching for fruit. The abundant food provided at wildlife refuges allows them to live in small family groups.

- Orangutans are highly intelligent primates. They share at least 97 percent of their DNA with humans, and are one of our closest animal relatives. In zoos, they have been taught to use sign language, touch-screen video games, and the visual aspects of video chat. They are also the only animals known to exchange gifts and return favors.

- Orangutans are critically endangered. The forests where they live are being logged to plant oil palms. Palm oil is used as a butter substitute in candies, pastries, and other processed foods. It is also used as a biofuel substitute for gasoline. When trees are chopped down, rescued orangutans are cared for in wildlife refuges, but long-term survival will require preservation of their natural forest homes.

Learn More About Orangutans

Online

Borneo Orangutan Survival Foundation: www.orangutan.or.id

Orangutan Conservancy: www.orangutan.com

Orangutan Foundation International: www.orangutan.org

Orangutan Outreach: www.redapes.org

Books

Eason, Sarah. *Save the Orangutan.* New York: Rosen Publishing Group/PowerKids Press, 2009.

Eszterhas, Suzi. *Orangutan.* Eye on the Wild. London: Frances Lincoln Children's Books, 2013.

Ganeri, Anita. *Orangutans.* A Day in the Life: Rain Forest Animals. Chicago: Heinemann Library, 2011.

Schuster, Gerd. *Thinkers of the Jungle.* Königswinter, Germany: H. F. Ullmann, 2008.

For Izabella and Jacob, and all the other children who love animals
—M. E.

For Jen, Kate, Laura, Tracy, and Christina, my loving kid-lit family
that cheers me on as I swing wild in the treetops, and carries me
back to the top when I fall
—R. K.

Author's Acknowledgments

I thank God for wild animals. Hugs to Curtis for accompanying me to Borneo, and to Nicole
and Amish for dog-sitting. Special thanks to Myra Garces-Bacsal for inviting me to the Asian
Festival of Children's Content in Singapore. I am profoundly grateful to Lim for a guided tour of
Semenggoh Wildlife Centre in Sarawak, Malaysia, and to the Orangutan Foundation International
and Borneo Orangutan Survival. Heartfelt gratitude to Janet S. Wong for reading an extremely
rough draft of this book. Deep gratitude to my amazing agent Michelle Humphrey, wonderful
editor Noa Wheeler, incredible illustrator Renée Kurilla, and to Laura Godwin, April Ward,
and the entire Henry Holt publishing team.

Henry Holt and Company, LLC, *Publishers since 1866*

175 Fifth Avenue, New York, New York 10010

mackids.com

Henry Holt® is a registered trademark of Henry Holt and Company, LLC.

Text copyright © 2015 by Margarita Engle

Illustrations copyright © 2015 by Renée Kurilla

All rights reserved.

Library of Congress Cataloging-in-Publication Data

Engle, Margarita.

Orangutanka : a story in poems / Margarita Engle ; illustrated by Renée Kurilla. — First edition.

pages   cm

Summary: All the orangutans are ready for a nap in the sleepy depths of the afternoon—all except one.

Written in a series of linked poems in the tanka style, an ancient Japanese form of poetry.

Includes bibliographical references.

ISBN 978-0-8050-9839-6 (hardback)

1. Orangutans—Juvenile fiction. [1. Orangutans—Fiction. 2. Familial behavior in animals—Fiction.

3. Naps (Sleep)—Fiction. 4. Waka.] I. Kurilla, Renée, illustrator. II. Title.

PZ10.3.E58397Or 2015   [E]—dc23   2014019224

Henry Holt books may be purchased for business or promotional use. For information on bulk purchases please contact the
Macmillan Corporate and Premium Sales Department at (800) 221-7945 x5442 or by e-mail at specialmarkets@macmillan.com.

First Edition—2015 / Designed by April Ward

The illustrations for this book were created with pencil and ink, and colored digitally.

Printed in China by Toppan Leefung Printing Ltd., Dongguan City, Guangdong Province

10 9 8 7 6 5 4 3 2 1